A Gift For:

____

From:

____

PUBLISHED BY HALLMARK GIFT BOOKS,
A DIVISION OF HALLMARK CARDS, INC.,
KANSAS CITY, MO 64141
VISIT US ON THE WEB AT HALLMARK.COM.

EDITORIAL DIRECTOR: DELIA BERRIGAN
ART DIRECTOR: CHRIS OPHEIM
ILLUSTRATOR: PAIGE BRADDOCK
DESIGNER: DAN HORTON

ISBN: 978-1-63059-964-5
HGN1215

MADE IN CHINA
APR16

Hallmark

IT'S THE GREAT PUMPKIN, CHARLIE BROWN™

BY CHARLES SCHULZ

As Halloween approached, Linus sat down to write his annual letter . . .

Dear Great Pumpkin, I am looking forward to your arrival on Halloween night. I hope you will bring lots of presents . . .

Charlie Brown thought Linus was crazy. Linus's sister, Lucy, thought so, too.

"You'll make me the laughingstock of the neighborhood!" she said.

Sally didn't think Linus was crazy. In fact, she decided she would join her sweet baboo in the pumpkin patch. They would wait for the Great Pumpkin to arrive together.

When he checked his mailbox, Charlie Brown was excited to discover an invitation to Violet's Halloween party.

"I've never gotten a party invitation before!" he said.

"Your name must have wound up on the wrong list," Lucy said. "You were on the *don't invite* list."

"Good Grief," Charlie Brown sighed.

On Halloween night, the gang set out in their costumes. Linus stayed behind in the pumpkin patch and invited the gang to sing pumpkin carols. Lucy didn't want to miss out on the fun and marched past him.

Sally thought about going trick-or-treating, but decided to stay with her sweet baboo.

Lucy pulled double trick-or-treat duty.

"It's so embarrassing to have to ask for something extra for that blockhead, Linus," Lucy complained.

"I got a chocolate bar," Pigpen said.

"I got a quarter!" Schroeder exclaimed.

"I got a rock," Charlie Brown sighed. Poor Charlie Brown got a rock at every house.

After trick-or-treating, the gang went to Violet's party. On the way, they saw Linus and Sally still in the pumpkin patch. They'd already missed trick-or-treating; would they miss the party, too? Did they really think the Great Pumpkin would show up? The other kids couldn't believe it.

"Just wait until the Great Pumpkin comes," Sally defended. "Linus knows what he's doing. The Great Pumpkin will be here!"

At the party, the gang listened to music and ate popcorn balls.

"Alright, alright, let's bob for apples," Lucy said.

HAPPY
HALLOWEEN

Back at the pumpkin patch, a shadowy figure was starting to rise up out from the pumpkins. Linus was so excited he fainted!

But it wasn't the Great Pumpkin. It was just Snoopy in his Halloween costume.

Linus woke up. "What happened?"

"I was robbed!" Sally yelled. "I spent the whole night waiting for the Great Pumpkin, when I could have been out for tricks or treats. Halloween is over, and I missed it!"

Sally went home and left Linus alone in the pumpkin patch.

“Well, another Halloween has come and gone,” Charlie Brown said the next morning. “I don’t understand it. I went trick-or-treating and all I got was a bag full of rocks.”

“And the Great Pumpkin never showed up?” he asked Linus.

“Nope,” Linus admitted.

“Well, don’t take it too hard, Linus. I’ve done a lot of stupid things in my life, too.”

“STUPID? What do you mean ‘stupid’? Just wait ’til next year, Charlie Brown. You’ll see! Next year at this same time, I’ll sit in that pumpkin patch until the Great Pumpkin appears. He’ll rise out of that pumpkin patch and he’ll fly through the air with his bag of toys. Just wait and see...”

Good grief, thought Charlie Brown.

If you have enjoyed this book
or it has touched your life in some way,
we would love to hear from you.

Please send your comments to:

Hallmark Book Feedback
P.O. Box 419034
Mail Drop 100
Kansas City, MO 64141

Or e-mail us at:
booknotes@hallmark.com